Franklin and the Tooth Fairy

ISBN 0-590-25469-3

Text copyright © 1996 by P.B. Creations Inc.
Illustrations copyright © 1996 by Brenda Clark Illustrator Inc.
Interior illustrations prepared with the assistance of Dimitrije Kostic.

24 23 22 21 20 19 18 17 16 15   9/9 0 1 2 3 4/0

Printed in the U.S.A.   23

First Scholastic printing, January 1996

Franklin and
the Tooth Fairy

Paulette Bourgeois
Brenda Clark

SCHOLASTIC INC.
New York   Toronto   London   Auckland   Sydney

FRANKLIN could count by twos and tie his shoes. He had lots of good friends, and one best friend, named Bear. Franklin and Bear were the same age. They lived in the same neighborhood. They liked the same games. But one morning, Franklin discovered a way that he and Bear were different.

Waiting for the school bus, Bear put his paw in his mouth and wiggled a tooth back and forth. It jiggled and wiggled and then, with a tug, it came out.

"Look at this!" said Bear. "I lost my first tooth."

Franklin was startled. There was even a little blood on the tooth. "That's terrible. How are you going to tell your mother?"

Bear laughed.

"My teeth are supposed to fall out," said Bear.
"It makes room for my grown-up teeth."

Franklin ran his tongue around his gums. They
were smooth and firm . . . and completely toothless.

"I don't have any teeth," said Franklin.

It was Bear's turn to be surprised.

Franklin's friends shook their heads sadly. "Too bad," they said.

Franklin wondered why. He had never needed teeth before.

Bear wrapped his tooth in a bit of tissue and put it in his backpack. "I need to keep this safe," he said.

All the way to school, Franklin wondered why Bear wanted to keep his old tooth. Especially if he was going to get a brand-new grown-up tooth. Now *that* was exciting.

"Why do you want to keep your tooth?" asked Franklin. "Won't you get a big one soon?"

All his friends looked at him with amazement.

"Don't you know about the tooth fairy?" asked Fox. Franklin shook his head.

"At night, before you go to sleep, you put your baby tooth under your pillow. Then the tooth fairy comes and takes the tooth away," explained Fox.

"But that's stealing," said Franklin. "Besides, what does the tooth fairy do with all those teeth?"

There was a long pause.

Bear scratched his head. Fox swished his tail, and Rabbit twitched.

"I don't know," said Bear, "but she always leaves something behind."

"One of her own teeth?" asked Franklin.

Everybody laughed.

"Oh, Franklin!" said Fox. "The tooth fairy leaves a present."

Franklin wondered what kind of present a tooth fairy would leave.

"I hope I get some money," said Bear.

"When I lost my first tooth, I got a new book," said Raccoon.

"I got crayons," Fox said.

Franklin rubbed his gums. He wished he had a tooth to leave for the tooth fairy. He wanted a present, too.

Bear showed his tooth to Mr. Owl as soon as he got to school.

Mr. Owl was very excited. "Losing your baby teeth means you are growing up," he said.

Franklin did not say anything. He had no teeth, but he wanted to feel grown-up, too.

Franklin was quiet for the rest of the day.

Even at home, Franklin was quieter than usual.

"What's wrong?" asked Franklin's mother.

"I don't have any teeth," he answered.

"Neither do we," said his father. "That's the way turtles are."

"But I want teeth," said Franklin.

His parents looked surprised.

"My friends get presents from the tooth fairy when they lose their teeth," said Franklin.

"Why do they get presents for old teeth?" asked Franklin's father.

"Because it means they are growing up," said Franklin.

"I see," said his father.

That night, just before bed, Franklin had a good idea. Perhaps tooth fairies did not know that turtles have no teeth. He found a tiny white rock to put under his shell.

He asked his mother to help him write a note. It read:

> *Dear Tooth Fairy,*
>
> *This is a turtle tooth. You may not have seen one before. Please leave a present.*
>
> *Franklin*

Franklin woke up very early the next morning. He looked under his shell. The rock was gone, but there was a note instead of a present.

He ran to his parents' room. "What does it say?" he asked.

Franklin's father put on his reading glasses.

Dear Franklin,

Sorry. Turtles don't have teeth.
Good try.

Your friend, The Tooth Fairy

Franklin was very unhappy until he noticed a big
wrapped package near his breakfast bowl.

"Open it," said Franklin's mother.

Inside was a beautiful book.

"Who is it from?" asked Franklin.

"From us," said his parents. "To celebrate your
growing up."

Franklin stood very tall. "Thank you."

From then on, Franklin didn't worry about being different from Bear. He knew that, in all the important ways, he and Bear were exactly the same.